# THOUGHTS IN A PENSIVE AUTUMN

MAHIBAH AHMED

This book is a compilation of poetries written over autumns of 2021 and 2022. Autumn is a pensive time, reflecting on the year that has gone past. It is a collection of 50 poems, divided into five sections: Change, This World, Life and Regrets, Memories and Under the Stars – all of which sum up the Autumn. It is about the excitement in the first leaf of autumn to the melancholy the afterthoughts sometimes bring. My poems also talk about the situation of war and peace in the modern world and strongly advocate peaceful methods instead of war. As a young poet, I want my poems to give message of peace and equality to create a better world for the generations to come. So, autumn can be full of regrets and joys, constraints and possibilities, and fear and hope at the same time – making it a roller coaster of emotions. I have tried to capture those thoughts, moments and fancies and penned them down in the form of poetry and compiled in this collection.

*Introduction*

A poetic collection of thoughts – warm and cold, through a pensive, somewhat eventful yet calm, changing yet pleasant, dying yet alive, dark yet lively, ending yet beginning, rustling but a wisely quiet autumn. These poems are composed over a silent September, bronze October, and grey and calm November of 2021 and 2022. Perspectives change in Autumn. It is not merely a dull quietness — it is a seed of peace and joy. Leaves fall only to rise again. A time to be pensive and re-analyze our experiences of the season that flies by — thoughtful while being pleasurable.

— Mahibah Ahmed

First Published by

An Imprint of BlueRose Publishers
**ISBN: 978-93-5704-978-8**
**BLUEROSE PUBLISHERS**
www.bluerosepublishers.com
info@bluerosepublishers.com

# Contents

*Dedicated to my maternal grandparents Saira Khatoon and Md Saleem Ahmad for their unconditional love and support at all times*

# CHANGE

### *I Saw the First Leaf of Autumn Fall*

I saw the first leaf of autumn fall
I heard the near winters call
And after one another follow
Till the tree is dry and hollow

Summer puts down its flowers
After times of warmth in a deep sleep
Autumn yellows the bowers
And under the gold carpet its treasure keeps

Yellow leaves turning red
And while that is being said
We see the time fly by
As on the old grass we lie

By the warmth the campfire gives
Memory of the past lives
Thinking the year as it flies
Like in spring a leaf, in autumn dies

Time flies in a wink of an eye
Frost, flowers, sun scurry by
Remember the moments as they dance
Around the campfire as they prance

They all are sweet and sour
Of yellow woods and spring bower
Rose's scents and ripening pears
Tooting owls and grizzly bears

The frost on the windows as winter lifts it's head
The crunch of the leaves as autumn on it treads
The flowers in the meadows green
The fruits on the trees have been

Look at the clouds go sailing by
As on the lush green grass we lie
The grass that wears dew of young winter
Yellowness of autumn and lush of summer

These are the shades nature wear
It too flips sides, is it queer?
Because in nature we lie
No matter how much we deny.

### *Sides of the Same Leaf*

The chills shivered the bare tree
To summer the snow is the key
The snow that settled on the branches old
Was into a million leaves unfold

Slowly the snow melted away to spring
And pleasure the blooming flowers did bring
And as the air grew warmer with time
The nature sang the summer rhyme

A leaf is born green
But all that has come and been
Decides the colour of the fluttering thing
The storm and dews the seasons bring

In summer the wind shakes the tree
And the dancing leaf nowhere rather be
The dust on top settles down
The winds blow and eases the frown

The leaves are warm and still
The air the sweet scents of roses fill
Not all that is good lasts forever
The shades seldom rest; stop never

The winds of chill shake the air
The wind is cold, the trees made bare
Dew drops settle on the top
And hurts it each raindrop

All the winds and the dews that have been
All the seasons the leaf had seen
Has made it yellow and red with time
And learnt life is neither a hill or a diamond mine

It's the top of the leaf that bears the scars
It's the side that saw the sun and chilly stars
It's still alive to remember and wait
The times there were and the fate

It seizes the opportunity to fly
Away and away to soar to the sky
It swirls and twirls in the air so open
One last time, memories and hopes hopen

It's the side that faced the sky and stood
Dark as night, strong as the bare wood

The side that was hidden from the grief
It is soft unlike the other side of the leaf

It's the seasons of life that make us all rare
It's the lush and alternating bare
So face the winds and let them blow
Never bow to it and it will go

And you too will rise again better
And your spirit nothing will deter
As the autumn leaves will have tales to tell
Of the world it saw before it fell

The life is a year of seasons queer
Of times of cold and spring's care
The time goes through paths you will love and dread
And each will pass and show more to tread.

## *Bound to Go*

The leaves change slowly but
We only know that autumn's here
When dahlia bloom and sparrow strut
They remind us that winter is near

The leaves change ever so softly
To crunch the second they fall
Till they leave go to their beds lofty
The dancing leaves enthral

How much in summer we wished
The flowers wouldn't go
But it's all the nature blissed
Upon us Autumn leaves bestow

Such a galliard is in the air
Of dancing winds and leaves
They spin around and they dare
To dance and gracefully end heave

I cannot stop the turning summer
Neither beg them to hold on
Because I know must come a winter
Nor can I deny the beauty in an autumn lawn

Time flies like winds in autumn
It freezes the soul like winter snow
It sings like the summer's rhythm
And seeds of hope like spring sow

Things come and go and over it
The power we have is none
After dark every path is lit
From every season's rising sun.

## Prelude to Spring

If all the year was a song
Autumn would be the best part
Summer short and winter long
And spring to warm the heart

Birds will sing the summer rhyme
Dry leaves make the autumn beat
Tingling snow sings of winter time
And the grace spring flowers meet

If all year was a long, sweet melody
Happiness summer would bring
As sweet is made sweeter by melancholy
Winter be the prelude to spring.

### *The Healer*

Scars of summer on the dry land
Desert and wind and blowing sand
The thunderstorm lasted a while
The heat from the burning fire is vile

All is lost, never to be recovered
Never in these trees leaves hover
All we had we lost to the unknown
Except that the burning fire, still shone

We looked at the burning grass and the sky
We remembered the pleasant times that passed by
If something could bring it into my world again
If only hope would rain, no, we will suffer in pain

The fire has died, our dreams burnt to ground
Ashes is all is there, to gaze we are bound
To gaze at our hopes crushed with the heat
To gaze at the dreams crushed by our own feet

Another morning lay before me
Another morning to just be
As summer fell into fall
Cold winds still enthral

Time passed and winter came
Hopeless, time is to blame
Nothing sows in the icy land
Nothing grows as truth lies in hand

All the year went sadly by
When once on the grass, on rock now we lie
Suddenly we heard the tune of spring
And birds and flowers it did bring

Happiness filled the air
The ground was no more bare
Grass grew under the feet
And pleasure the eyes did meet

There is one thing to remember in pace
Fall and spring comes due to time's grace
There is one thing to remember for all
Time is the greatest healer of all.

## *I Went to See the Cherry Tree*

I returned to the spring tree
It got forgotten some day
And some passing dream brought it to me
As over work I lazily lay

I walked on the path I once did tread
It was dry, not green like I thought
It was still warm, the hope wasn't dead
It seemed in forgotten memories it got caught

The tree stood there despite the cold
Dry leaves laid still on the ground
Its branches were frail and old
Under its branches old memories found

The floor was wet with the mud
No green grass as I remembered
There wasn't a hope or a bud
It wasn't flowering as I rendered

The wind was dry and the sky was grey
It didn't feel cold though, it was warm still
I remembered each spring under it I lay
It was dead, that was it, my eyes with tears did fill

I walked back home a little sad
I wished I could save the tree
Now memories were all I had
But can good hope let that be?

On that sad windy day
I thought I would start again
I stole a piece of heart away
And placed it away from the memory lane

I thought I would start anew
I kept it in the morning light
On it settled the winter dew
I wished the hope would heal the sight

It was days later I saw snow melt
I saw the ground clear and grass peek
Warm in the still cold air I felt
It was the first word spring did speak

In memories the world was so sweet
No troubles, no deaths, and no grief

Where did they go? Burnt in time's heat?
Just like the blossom and the leaf

The shone bright, the grass was green
The chirps came back, the life anew
The nature its garden did preen
The nature now wore a different hue

On one half-forgotten day
I saw a little plant longing for gaze
It was the little stowaway
And in spring it's green did daze

There were a lot more spring,
And winters, summers, and rains
And birds, hid and lay and did sing
And a lot more trips down the memory lane

And then many springs after all
I found the one for which I did wait
Finally, I saw a cherry blossom fall
To bloom and rise again is the fate

I remembered all the autumns and spring
And all that that had come and been
To me pleasure it always brings
To realise that more of life had I seen

The memory lane was longer now
A simple kind act done in the past
No matter where or when or how
Can many long winters last

I sat under the tree once again
Warm it did bring me
I remembered the many winters away the pain
I felt but then let hope be

It's was not immortal bloom
It went and came and passed
Neither was immortal the gloom
Longing for the spring it kept me till last

That old winter was so full of gloom
I made mistakes, lamented, and fixed them away
And now as I remember the new old cherry tree bloom
All because I hoped and dreamt on one cold winter day.

## Autumn Springs

The sky is getting greyer and colder
For the leaves a beautiful death, bolder
Under the grey sky, the blue-sky recall
Autumn springs as summer fall

Summer paints gardens lush
Autumn paints warm unlike the rush
And then wetted the dry leaves green once
It begins its cold winds under the hiding suns

Sunlight paling through the window
Raindrops and autumn leaves settle low
It may feel dark by the graves, in the empty halls
But it is just autumn springing as summer fall

And leaves may fall and sky may grey
And the trees put on but a green display
Summer wins hearts and it calls
Autumn springs as summer falls.

### *How Change Changes with Change*

A thousand flowers it has seen
A million more leave have been
A petal falls upon the ground
But the fair nature's bound

As what goes up
Must come down
What goes down must rise again
Like in spring the trees in lane

A petal falls as start not end
Leaves fall as a change not bend
Winter comes but to give life
So that in spring the flowers can thrive

Spring comes but to cherish
Gifts winter gave before it's perished
Summer arrives only so
That winter shall come and cover it with snow

Winter arrives to give new life
Under the snow testing new strife
Only then rises the best
After winter's toughest

Spring again arrives
To encourage the budding lives
As what comes down rises
As nature its plan devises

What gives the spring its glory
Are the winds it left behind shivery
What makes a diamond so fine
Is the pressure and dark it left behind

All once shivered shall have glory
All once down shall rise
Unfold itself will the mystery
As the nature it's plan devise.

### *Immortal Spring*

In the glory of the winter's sweep
All is covered in the dying earth
All is sealed in a slumber deep
Waiting for the time it's worth

The leaves fall but the spirits don't
The wind blows and the cold bites
Forget the forbidden falls I won't
And the crimson views from the heights

The air is dull but not gloomy yet
As autumn rain in my ears ring
I realised as on the wet grass I tread
In my soul lives an immortal spring.

### *Maple Skies*

The skies change due to obligations eternal
The birds come out to their chores diurnal
The leaves fall and glide in the cold air
The boats come back from whence they fared

In the autumn's soar as the sky ages
I pen down these verses on crisp pages
Sky wears the best shades of ash grey
This memory will someday make my day

The sunsets are darker now as cold sets in
The orange rays paint the grey over it's sins
The yellow rises from the setting sun
The rose hues of autumn blend as one

On the back of the wind autumn leaps
Crimson maples besides stars it keeps
Covering the sky in rose and golden hues
As my maple violin a sweet melody sews

And now I sit and contemplate and remember
How close seems the coming and last December
Memories circle around and time flies I realise
Nothing is here to stay, not even these maple skies.

### *Mortal Green*

I planted this maple in an autumn field
And no green leaves yet it did yield
There was but a tender foliage
And drying things formed in a cage

Slowly summer slipped in the scene
And the tree put on a display of green
And the warm breeze whispered through
The alive new leaves of a greener hue

Summer went well and I thought it would be
Like this forever in the field of eternal green
But wrong was I proved by the seasons queer
Once what was green was found nowhere

Should not have loved a thing so much
That it was hard to let go of memory's clutch
I regret all that I didn't see before
I regret that I didn't care to see more

And now in my tired cold hands
When I guessed I had lost my chance
I realised that seasons change and iron rusts
And watched as the leaf crumbled to dust.

## *November*

November mist has now settled in
I'm afraid these maple skies have to go
Though this autumn many hearts did win
The rise has now come to a low

I look back on my verses,
Written, unwritten and wished
All my blessings and curses
Times I regretted and cherished

Now the mist doesn't lift for evenings
Only lets sun break through at dawn
And the lavender drops are condensing
On every rose petal in the morn

The sky a darker shade now
The wind a swifter beast
Before the wind the shades bow
Now I remember the most and the least

The autumn is now slipping away
Through the thin veils of seasons
I regret not knowing it straightaway
Not knowing, not all things have a reason.

# This World

### *What heals?*

The world is broken
Disputes awoken
Withering away is the peace
Past repeats itself, future on lease

Will time heal it or mess it?
Will there be a lamp or candle lit?
Are we doomed to doom?
In our minds the pasts loom

Time does not heal
The pain of parting it doesn't feel
Our grieves and wishes don't go away
But we get used to living with it each day

Whose content in grief?
Whose solitude in a dying leaf?
Who saves mankind this time?
The past, future, present...time?

## *Mortal men, Immortal Wars*

As the sun burns a spirit will be awaken
The world into two parts broken
Though fragmented already will do it again
The same pain felt, down the same old lane

The springs will be silent
The battlegrounds will be violent
The sands immortal blood-stained
And thousands of soldiers maimed

And many thousand more brave
Lie under the green grass in grave
Humanity kills itself and dies
And rises, consoles, promises but lies.

## *Immortal Wars*

Peace is hard due to something sweet
It is memories and heartfelt retreat
And we want to extend the hand for you
But the past holds us back, what do I do?

Blood is immortal once shed
People are immortal once dead
And we want to come together yet
The past holds for you a greater debt

People are trapped in the ancient cages
Ancientness is trapped in modern ages
Peace is killed in the wars once mortal
And now peace is not immortal

The feelings of revenge hold us back
The strength to rise above it we lack
We would love to put aside the quarrel
But mortal wounds will hurt immortal

And hence this vicious cycle again
Mistakes, forgiveness, war and pain
The torch with the new age is held high
The Immortals wars must die.

## *Give Time Some Time*

Time flies for you and me
Justice unfair for strong and weak
Truth lies beyond land and seas
Some unconventional truth I seek

In the world the wars were infinitely waged
And the bruise of the past still bleeds
The ideas and emotions by borders caged
And yet here we stand in a world without peace

I know it's hard to feel and conceal
I know the rage like the tides ebb and swell
I know the bruises of the past are hard to heal
But it's about time, you give time some time as well.

## *Citizen of this World*

Our world, is a mere piece of land
Divided it falls, together it stands
And yet it is so broken that it is not one
Held by the sword, ruled by the gun

They are all in the same run
Under same rain, moon and Sun
They use the same bricks to make their wall
The same walls that we make fall

The same 'hard' goes in their work
The same fears about them lurk
The same words of kindness they say
Under the same sky and stars they lay

As one mankind claims the sun
We conquered the height with quarrels none
Together we made our astonishing feats
And so when you defeat it, the world is defeated

If we all belong to not one
But all the lands under the sun
And in every heart the same hope curled
Peacefully we are citizens of this world.

## *Here We Fall*

Through the many tales of old
Changes brought but freedom sold
In money we trust; money leads deeds
And no sold man a free air need

The wars were fought and people torn
Amid the old chaos nations born
To strive to honour freedom above gold
Dreaming for years only to be sold

Ideals of the past to time are lost
Money now comes at moral's cost
The blood still stains the sand of ages
People are stuck in unseen cages

People, nations, land did money divide
The true meaning of humanity died
No more of losing honour is the fear
It's only hoarded gold that is held dear

The world is warming with hate's heat
To gold mankind has accepted defeat
Lands have been divided enough by wall
The world has risen enough to fall.

### *Empires Die on the Other Side of the Fence*

Through time we have seen
That phenomenon has been
Nothing remains of empire
But dust, and mud and fire

In the broken lands jilted
Peer through the fences, flowers wilted
To rise, falling is the fate
And what breaks land, is hate

These iron needles in quilts who weaves?
Men can mingle like autumn leaves
What breaks them then is hate unsaid
And that is what makes empires dead

Why dead empires don't rise
Why trust comes as disguise
Is why we befriend and trust and again
We go down the same lane; same pain

The same kind can't hate each other
We cannot forbid our brother
On the other side of the fence,
Suffers our kind, we call it defence!

It is not that people hate each other
Or divided want to be the brother
It is just a wave of hate that carries us
And when we look back, it is all dust

What is the use of empires or power?
If you win-a hero, seek peace- you cower
If you can claim your innocent fellows as defence
Worse, can't console'em on the other side of fence

When you kill your fellows, you don't win
People don't hate from within
Empires don't fall due to conflicts intense
They die on the other side of the fence.

## *Ink bleeds*

White papers, scribbled words
Turn yellow, unfathomed, untouched
Ink flows but clots at the thought
Of writing about a world tainted by war
Painted by glory and laden with gold
Not a day goes without the doubt
That somewhere in this land is human suffering
A suffering so unknown to the elite
And so known to those in plight
That the differences between them widens, deepens
Regrets, thoughts, tears shed, blood shed
Cuts mark the graves of the unknown
Inks bleed like blood in the paper's bone
All the world is a stage said Shakespeare
I wonder if I am my own scriptwriter
Or if God wrote the script of this entire world
Can't we make it a little brighter?

## *Clock*

Seconds, minutes, hours, tick away
Anger burns itself in its own fiery fumes
The fire that only the wildest can desire
To look in eyes, to feel, to burn, to waste away in
To have the knowledge that all you have
May or will ever own is not yours but
They are the seeds sown in the universe's feet
And are never yours because they all tick away
Memories fade like the north star on a hazy night
And all we hold onto is the ardent brilliance of
The pieces of soul we hold and hold dear through plights
And the heartaches all become undiminishable stars
That we look upon each day as we have left them a far
And oh! What a petite thing is a harmless clock that ticks and tocks
And never stops but this very thing is the one that has been
The reason for the ending of lives, memories, fates, eternities.

## *Tomorrow*

Long winters and endless pains have plagued
This world of ours, and shattered it like glass
And in this hour, all the tainted glory it wears
Are all the broken fragments we piece together
To make a life out of the bleeding past
Oddly coloured, oddly shaped, oddly stained glass
And all the times they lost hope, starved, fought, died
And all the times graves were too many for this land
And all the times that ancient pains were revived
We hoped against hope for a tomorrow where we held hands
When we lost all that, we had and all we didn't
When they knew that this war will last and won't end for ages
When the sun didn't shine and the end did hint
We hoped for a tomorrow where this was just verse on pages
Seldom do such mere hopeful possibilities exist
That give a flicker of hope to all human sufferings
Things will one day get better, yes, if you persist
Through all the times of war and peace and holy sins
Tomorrow may be a better day for hopes and dreams
Tomorrow may be a better day to leave it all in history
Tomorrow may be a better day, bless this curse, redeem
Tomorrow may be a better day to set fire to the fury
All this world has ever known is war and peace and that
Eternities pass, bloody hours pass, past is in the past
When wars would be waged at the mere drop of a hat
But tomorrows will keep us hoping till the last.

# Life and regrets

## *Fear*

The dark is cast and everyone sees in it
Everyone sees it but never the same
A devilish memory and not a candle lit
From the unknown past it came

Fears bound your feet with ropes unseen
It holds you back from your unlived dream
Millions of chances have come and been
It's the bounding fear in fury that gleam

Leap over the giant crack
That fear makes seem deeper
The courage to do is what one lacks
The greater the heaven feels the steeper

If you can walk down again the dreariest path
And not be half as scared as you were before
Then you may be empty handed but, in your heart,
You found the courage in an endless soar.

### *Prisoner of the past*

It free and yet it seems to bound
They say you can fly yet on the ground
Can't let go of the things that'd been
And blinded by it yet all is seen

Lives there in gloom and tears
And to step out it can't dare
That's the melancholy it cast
All upon the prisoner of the past.

## *Destined or fated*

I walked along the dark river bank
The water rippling, sparkling clanked
I sighed at the something I wished to know
Was I really me or there was more?

Was I a bird flying above the Ocean, daring
Or was I a poor sailor through life, sea faring
Was I the lucky one who had it all?
Then why did I feel like an empty wall?

Was I destined to be the best?
Or was I destined to be the worst?
Or will I ever see the world and fly?
Or was it all just hopes passing by

I fall like a broken leaf
I fail and then I heave
Like crumbled dust I rise
It is not long before the hope dies

I got up the dawn was breaking
My hopes were sore and I was aching
I had got my answer from a distinct call;
I was none of them, but had to be them all.

## *Seasons of grief*

I planted my very own tree of grief
Upon it my grieves wearily hung
And each leaf was still as fresh
Each day more leaves on it strung

It was spring for it I suppose
The leaves fluttered young
And I don't usually grief oppose
Except every day through mind they rung

Now they flourished so hard that,
Every branch in leaves was covered
And I wouldn't usually mind that as I sat
Except over my head the gloom hovered

Unbearable Summer I presume the new stage
Some leaves burnt but most renewed
And I wouldn't really mind the cage of rage
Except it left no room for joyous solitude

Now under my tree hopeless was I
The roots were strong and wind was cold
And noticed, some leaves were beginning to die!
I would never mind freedom from gloom's hold

I heaved and let the cold settle in
The leaves fell till there was but one
Autumn and winter perhaps let me win
I hoped and then, there were none.

## *Time lost*

We have lost the time we were given
We want but possibly can't fill
For moments lost, ourselves we have forgiven
But deep down its longed for still

For memories were once alive
A year ago turned decades
For what we just saw as spring arrive
Into a cold leaf has decayed

Still we look up to the grey sky
We try to patch the lost time
And as we do time is still flying by
Whether you trick it or pay a million dime

Lost cannot be recovered
Nor turn the hands around
For ages this lament has hovered
Still to go time is bound

The fabric of time has been tainted
We suffered and have laments, and will
And no matter how many times it's painted
Time lost, is longed for still.

## *Lost in lost time*

The realities now will be twisted
When future arrives with its residents
The wrongs and goods all be listed
But still never remembered, seen and went

Some thing's are better said than done
Some truths better never said
Some victories are better never won
Deeds once done though are never dead

Some things better never told
Some times better kept secrets
Some times better not issues hold
Yet if done they will cause no regrets

Words, worlds, past: all fades away
No restrains should come at regrets cost
And somewhere in wandering time they lay,
Somewhere, sometime, lost in time now lost.

## *Lying Truths*

All beliefs aren't true
Lies also lie in a lighter hue
Truth takes refuge in shadows
The quiet truth eternal lies sows

The lies find abode in darker shades
The concealed truth in light fades
Whole lies still a sober die
But half-truth are worse lies

All the truth is a belief I say
All worse lies will be truth one day
As when they hold truth guilty of lies
That is the day when all the truth dies

Truth and lies both come at pain
One of heart and one of brain
To tell the truth is truly good indeed
But to tell a lie is a worse worldly need

All the truths and lies are a belief
All words are worth is joy or grief
Hence today all the truth that gleams
Tomorrow won't be as true as it seems.

### *Floating Dreams*

This river bed of fate is where
The orange maples of autumn float
To places unknown these drops fare
And down this rocky stream sails life's boat

There are waves and eddies and swirls
That cover the somewhat rough stream
It is a leap of faith and a ride of whirls
As in her crystal waters born are dreams

Some dreams live, some never find shore
All are meant for different sailing boats
All are made for different sailor's core
And each new wave a new story quotes

In these parts of the water rocky and steep
Is where all the desires and disasters unfurl
Unknown are the secrets these ripples keep
Unknown are the clams that have the pearl

In these unstable ways of the waves
New dreams each day hearts weaved
Each day new tracks in the waters they pave
To scale how far hope and faith can lead.

*Autumn Rains on my Soul*

Autumn rains are here again
But I still feel last autumn's pain
New drops fall now from the sky
But still old regrets they bring by

I remember every word under this roof
I remember all the times I spent aloof
When it may have been better together
When it wasn't raining out of the weather

The tinkles on the roof tap my heart
And my regrets like bleeding blood start
To forget them now is said to be wise
But to say so is like wearing a disguise

Autumn rains tap my soul once more
I wonder if the past a different story bore
Would it make it better now as leaves sweep
Or would these grieving clouds still weep

I remember those summer skies
And with that all the beautiful lies
I remember those magical sights I saw alone
Instead with you when you weren't gone

Autumn rains, I can never part
With your echoes in my heart
Remind me of the regrets away had I locked
Before on my soul the raindrops knocked.

### *Graceful Falls*

Like the drying autumn leaves
I crumble—
As the flower petal heaves
I wilt—
As the stars no more align
I lose myself—
As the wind is no more mine
I settle—
I fall, I regret, I rise and forget
The dreary deserts and oceans past
I wish I could not crumble to dust, fumble in my moment
Jumble the things I put together for this moment
But the springs awakens, the old petals shaken
The constellation shifts and the defeated wind lifts
The sands cool down, hear the old wave's sound
The phases of the moon, heal the old wound
Alas! At last! I guess glory was not always at this height
When I falter, I fall, I fail in my fight
Then I rise like tides on a full moon night.

# Memories

### *Forgotten Halls*

Once more I tread on these empty halls
Once more I hear the distant wild calls
These wooden patterns that once were known
Seem strange now that I have long gone

These frosty windows that I gazed through
Upon the spring gardens and summer dew
In these candle lit halls I remember
The smell of rain and burning timber

Within these walls I spent many springs
And still warmth in my heart memories bring
At cold nights I lie listening to the clock
And gazing out the window at the sparrow flock

In the middle of nowhere, trees tall as sky
I can see dancing memories go by
I retrace every curve in the mahogany doors
I remember by the fire the fantastic lores

Now as leaves fall and there is nothing to do
I return to the place where my memories I sew
The leaves pile the locked door now so old
Withered by the wind, past in its folds

Now in this time I have come once more
To look for the memories the old wood bore
To feel what was once felt by me
To halls of comfort I turn the key.

## *All we really own*

In memory of time flown past
In wait of things unseen
In a world where moments last
Just as long as a dream so lean

In times we carry in our heart
We know how good it feels
To remember and carry a part
In your little heart ever-sealed

I remember the fading stars alight
On the sky of the brightening dawn
Now though the road is a winding sight
I still remember the sweet moments gone.

## *Eternal Memories*

Our souls' mysteries surround
Hearts our memories bound
And wish to turn is yet another pain
All efforts and trudges sink in vain

We made mistakes and yes, we lament
Remember the soulful cries that went
The laughter in the little things once found
And that free day when no obligations bound

We remember the aches
The past who makes
With its bitters and sweets and sours
Which is sad, joyous, mixed yet ours

Nothing remains of us but dust
Nothing remains of iron but rust
Remains are the resonance of our voice
And the old lifeless things that we rejoice

What remains of you is not a part,
It is the honour in the world's heart
In the graves lie we, our wrongs and dream
Let the reminisce in every heart us redeem

We cannot fix the tainted past
Even souls cannot time outlast
Rethinking past bears no gain
Time lost is never found again

After we die in our deep graves we lie
Our dreams, desires, failures we can't deny
Our life and wrongs we may ourself forgive
But certainly, in eternal memories they live.

## Memories Trudging By

Deeper dark has covered the air
The leaves are fallen; trees bare
The soft once now crunch dead
As over it the weary boots tread

The wind is calm; the air so still
The leaves rustle on the autumn hill
Everything is dead, the leaves, the trees
There is still some hope in the tired knees

Admire the crops that flutter like gold
On a dark night so still, so cold
Admire the old giving way to new
As on each fallen leaf settles the dew

All is gone: the lush, the green
Once plump became thin and lean
We seem to have lost all we grew
All except the sweet warming few

Remember when the dry was green
Remember flowers that have been
When on these trees there were leaves
When every warm wind a blessing heave

We haven't lost all the times
It's in our heart, in summer rhymes
They are still warm to help us through
The winter gloom and the darker hue

And when it all blossoms into spring
And more flowers and thoughts it brings
The sweetest of them all will be
The memories trudging by the winter tree.

***Kites Flown Past***

I gazed upon them hued kites
Where the sun shone bright
Now the evening is dark but still
I lazily gazed by my window sill

Where have those kites gone?
Where are the rays of dawn?
Where are those twinkling lights?
And the wind that lifted my kite?

I daydreamed by the hazing sight
Of the colourful fancies formed as kites
In the blue sky they soared without effort
Their presence didn't mind but absence hurts

Gone are the colours from the sky
How fast the summer flew by
Now there is nothing there but grey
Still waiting on kites by my window I lay.

## *Slip, Slip Away*

Under the tree trunk I rest my head
And feel the old leaves on my face
As I see my dead flowers go to bed
Before I could style them in a vase

And all those blue white potteries
That I collected for this day
Has served me with this mystery
As to believe again or trash it away

And I cannot, never again be
What I once thought I would
I can never, and never again see
The beauty in a dying wood

Don't let this moment slip away
Don't let the heaven or hell know
That in this body where a soul did lay
Has now left it for good, to go

Don't let this moment slip, slip away
Don't let the petals of these roses wilt
Don't let the pain numb your hands
And let me pass as soft as spinning silk

Would you not tell me what you think
Of me and care about this hour
Before the eternities slip away like
My now wilting summer flowers.

## *Fly East, Dear Birds!*

I saw a flock of a thousand birds of a feather
Fly through the autumn mist due to the weather
And gently flap their milky white wings through the day
To sail and map their way as if around the milky way

Fly east, gentle birds! And return not till spring
And over the hills and under the moons you sing
Until you reach your second abode of old
To help you survive the dreadful cold

Fly east, dear birds! I will see you once again
In this very clearing, in this very old lane
That now is dead with deadening winds and ivy
That then will be full of bright, bursting Bougainvillea

Fly east, dear bird! And fear you not these dangers
They will come your way and lands only get stranger
But remember the spirit in your cold beating heart
Fly through lavender skies like a moonstone arc

Fly east, young birds! And fare these seas a-far and gone
And let lores of fantasy and faith and truth be your song
Fly through the mists and valleys and oceans and when
You come and have learnt and are older tell me about them

Fly my birds! And be agile and faster than the wings of fairies
And down under the darkest night no matter how eerie
Be faster than the wind, desire burning like fire, warm heart
Though I may no more be when you return, I shall never part

Fly east my birds! Remember the way and times
Remember all the memories we made in rhymes
Feel the folklores of this land and take them where you roam
Let the memory of this quiet place lead you back home.

## *Fade*

Heart aches, winter pains, dawn breaks
Summer fades, spring arrives, autumn lakes
Leaves break free from the trees and summer
Comes and fades then autumn shades
Leaves dancing on the surface of lakes
When from the summer autumn breaks
Winter will forever come and feel like eternity
And stars come and stars disappear
Constellations shift forever and I fear
Heart aches, winters, dawns, rhymes,
Summers, springs, autumns, stars, dusk
Lakes, trees, eternities, mystical times,
Wind, love, constellations, reverberations must—
Fade.

### *Sunflower Wreaths*

I thought that was the life
By the meadow on a summer day
When gentle wind eased through fresh grass
And a mellow scent filled the air
And the soft petals of sunflower strangled
Between my fingers and my hair
And each bud as big as the heart I have
Each flower a burning gold flare
And gentle petals, wrinkled, soft, mortal
And yet it's memories so stiff and eternal
And the leaves a glossy green and they melt
Between my fingers as I try to string them
I try to sew some memories between each
Steal a rock of a soul I never owned
And place it between my flowers that
I string each summer daydreaming all alone
String them right and string them through
To make a crown that the moon could wear
And now there is nothing left on the barren field
That I could ever come back to and smile about
Nothing that I could string and wait on spring and
Fill my head with the warm sunflower air
There is no scent left in the air when I breathe
All I own now lives inside a dying sunflower wreath.

## *Farewell*

Farewell old friend and we may never meet
It was the end and you're gone and can't come
Pensively sometimes I do think if things
Were different then what would have changed
What could possibly be harmed if time was turned
And by some miracle you returned and nothing
Happened and I did not have to force this belief that
It was the end and you'd be here and no grief
And I still regret not seeing you when I had
The chance to and not being the best I could
And play your best music and dance to it and sing
Like childhood friends do and all the times I thought
That all the joy in the world could be bought
Vanished all at once when I knew
And all the times I tried to believe that I may
Never see you again, not today, not any day
And when I walk down that lane again
I will never be able to forget that autumn's pain
I will always hold the times we had together
All our moments through all weather
When you told me that I was smart and
All the art and mischiefs that ended bad
And all the dangerous bicycle rides and
All the stupid made up childish games
And all the talk of the wind and tide and
All the fights and all the blames for they
Light up who we were and will be always
We were friends through all times
That came and went
I can never forget those days and the day I knew
About that mortal accident.

# Under the Stars

## *Sound of silence*

The evenings are quiet
As quiet as quiet can be
Not a stirring in the sight
As dark as the night can see

The leaves leave their canopy
And come to rest on the forest floor
Covering it in vermillion hues
As souls rejoice in autumn's soar

Not a stirring upon this November
Not a sound like silent spring
Not a ray of light from ember
The autumn silence does bring

I walked upon a million roads
All as quiet as dark before dawn
In the dreams a million abodes
For the souls that believe in calm

There is this voice that goes unheard
As I lean on the old fence
I feel it yet goes unexpressed in words:
I feel the sound of silence.

## *Grieving Spirits*

At midnight under the autumn moon
The graveyard comes to life
And busy white forms that go away by day
Rejoice under the moonlight

They answer thy questions olden
And ponder new ways of giving
Take pride in their mere existence
And grieve and lament the living

How medieval things were fancies
How ancient artefacts grew
Out of the vintage bricks and ivies
To the fire and steel of the new

Out of all the questions ancient
One of them rises again and again
What if all the times magnificent
Were there's and not all their pains

They believe that all their eulogies
Were far too short for their time alive
And all their mistakes in miseries
Are too long to bear in after life

So maybe all the good done by them
Is burnt by the sun against their will
But all the bad they did not intend
Is preserved under the moonlight chill

All the times they had once loved and lost
All the times they waited by the window sill
Is still written on their epitaph in autumn frost
And all their wishes penned in ink on their will

All the good that they did in their path
Is now buried nowhere to be found
And now people talk about them in wrath
Now all their memory is deep underground

All the thoughts of how they had been
Or could have, sends shivers down the bones
As all the wrongs they did not mean
Are now engraved on their grave stones.

## *Dark Fancies*

I now see the winter light
Breaking through the trees
I stop to take in the sight
Before I take up a new adventure
To an unknown place I turn the key

The winter light does not lead
Much into the darkest wood
I feel a compulsion to regret my deed
I want to change the past now written
I bet I can, I wish I could

Not much comes out of this gloom
Not much has been in as well
So I may risk, may myself, doom
To see the probability of me coming out
After believing a heaven out of hell

I don't hold this belief to be true but
The dark is colourful in secret
As a river of crimson blood flows in the cuts
In my heart, the breaks in my soul
I believe it is made of regrets

I don't really fancy much glitter
But I may fancy mysterious dark
For in the sweet things there's bitter
As in the bitter there is always sweet
In the unknown there is a mysterious spark

In the core of my heart I will forever feel
The silver arcs of the moon a norm
In the shade of the light dark is still real
As the dreams in my fantasy of skies
All my words are in dark fancies formed.

## *Little Big Things*

Stare wide eyed into the night
And the infinite dark skies
Though the stars are at a certain height
I can feel them with my eyes
Don't just look at the stars
And forget about where you are
There they lay in the dark flowing
Robe of the universe, glittered sparks
Above all wars, all claims, all gold, all crowns
They let their brilliant ardency seep down
All these human movements and worries
Seem so small compared to the universe
Where all this wide world is just a dot
And non-existent are blessings and curses
All the reasons of wars and peace, tides
Low and high, gentle rain and morning breeze
Are so insignificant and so unknown.
The direction in which winds are blown
Are so not cared for in this galaxy
Yet they mean everything to the sailors returning home
So little is the sound of gentle pouring rain
But they make a great portion of rainy days
And the memories and all its pains
So little is the memory of autumn kites
Yet they are the most memorable flights
So little are sunflower wreaths compared to stars
Small bursting petals and big balls of fire
But these little things are all human heart desires
So small is the mere memory of a forgotten hall
Yet they are so big and dear to the hearts of all
We are small, insignificant, unknown in this universe
We are all the same, on the same little blue marble,
Our mere existence a marvel, our world is a chaos
We harbour. A chaos we harbour, in our little souls
In our little stages and people with little roles
We may be small but it is all so big and it matters
Where fire burns, ice freezes, glass shatters
These are the little big things that will always
And always keep this huge cosmos running
It's our little deeds that matter in a huge universe
Our little words, framed as deep poetic verse.

## *Fireflies*

Lead me into the light and dark and
All the hues the midnights spark when
Stars are hidden behind unknown canopies
And the wind a treacherous dance
When the blindfolded eyes can see nothing
Numb skins and hearts feel nothing
When the hands of ours do nothing
When you don't want to see but just glance
And stare into the darkness like the beauty to the beast
And dance around the exhausted fire patch
When I feel like my soul cannot light these skies
Take my hand and lead me, wild fireflies.

## Constellations Shift

Last winter under this sky I told a star
"Roses grow amidst the thorns"
I don't know if I followed that.
Last spring under that sky I told north star
"Autumn doesn't defy spring's glory"
Last summer I promised those stars
"Canopies don't bend before storms"
Last autumn I told my stars
"Dry flowers live on to tell the story"
Now under these stars I ask myself
Why did I prick myself, hide behind,
Bend in storms, fade away, break promises?
But it isn't just me that falters and lifts and lies
In this sky, constellations shift all the time.

## *Unconventional Compasses*

North star, constellations a-far, lead me through the night
And though you may be the unconventional ones
I am one of you too so I trust you to lead me right
And all the dreams I have ever owned
I have owed all my hopes and yearnings to you
And all of them I believe to be written in stars
And I have faith that my wishes will come true
And I string my daydreams into the whimsical veils of the night
That gather morning dew by the breaking dawn
Pearls, gentle pearls, they make a spectrum out of white light
I gaze at these Norway skies, like a child into the moon
And see the cold burning ribbons of aurora
Streaking, flashing, but its glory's death be soon
So venture will thee, into the open seas, and never return
To witness this familiar care, to breath this familiar air
As now for once and now for all I put conventions to burn
So guide me, tomorrow's sun, and this midnight's moon
Map my way along the oceans and through crimson deserts
Lead me well and lead me right to dreams and starry dunes
Yes, they change; Yes, they falter; Yes, they are hard to prophesize
Don't tell me this world is all conventions when the magic's still alive.

# Star Maps

These glittering sparks in the dark skies
Under the ones I lay on a moon lit meadow
Scattered like gentle drops of white lies
Fathom them into constellations by my window

Where was that star on the day you came,
On the day you left, the day I was born and died?
Maybe I was right or wrong but time is to blame
I believe that the conventional signs have lied

North star, lead my way to my dreams
And don't you leave a step on a cloud
These dreamy dark skies endless seems
For the farers the glowing night brought about

Map these stars on my hands in ink
Plot these skies on the papyrus eternal
Let them know when these stars link
Stars don't shift in their courses nocturnal

When these stars align and the sky is like this
When the wind is mine and let it be
When a night not full of regrets is a bliss
Sit by my window and remember me

Light up the sky, our promises and trust
Feel the stars rise and set and fade
Promises are broken but they never rust
And are as true to soul as wind to everglade

Plot the star map of the day I came and went
And the day that I thought I would surely die
The days I stood to the wind and days I bent
Paper maps crumble but star maps don't lie

Sail away into the milky way and no one knows
Where you are or want to go or going to be
In my mind a solitary river of fancies flows
And get lost in it to sea of tranquillity

Stars forever keep changing and the skies
Will move for eternities too many to count
A Soul lives and loves and rejoices and dies
Memories more than the whole sky amount.

*Then autumn shall rise again, like tides on a full moon night and maple leaves will fly again like hued kites through the autumn skies. Till then, farewell!*

www.ingramcontent.com/pod-product-compliance
Lightning Source LLC
LaVergne TN
LVHW091220180726
843490LV00007B/2861